The Busy Lunch

Level 2H

Written by Melanie Hamm
Illustrated by Stefania Maragna

Ticktock

What is synthetic phonics?

Synthetic phonics teaches children to recognise the sounds of letters and to blend (synthesise) them together to make whole words.

Understanding sound/letter relationships gives children the confidence and ability to read unfamiliar words, without having to rely on memory or guesswork; this helps them progress towards independent reading.

Did you know? Spoken English uses more than 40 speech sounds. Each sound is called a *phoneme*. Some phonemes relate to a single letter (d-o-g) and others to combinations of letters (sh-ar-p). When a phoneme is written down it is called a *grapheme*. Teaching these sounds, matching them to their written form and sounding out words for reading is the basis of synthetic phonics.

Consultant

I love reading phonics has been created in consultation with language expert Abigail Steel. She has a background in teaching and teacher training and is a respected expert in the field of Synthetic Phonics. Abigail Steel is a regular contributor to educational publications. Her international education consultancy supports parents and teachers in the promotion of literacy skills.

Reading tips

This book focuses on the sounds from level 2:
sh, ch, th as in them, th as in thin, ng, nk, le.

Tricky words in this book

Any words in bold may have unusual spellings or are new and have not yet been introduced.

Tricky words in this book:

has the of no I we
need goes to he wood
chairs hay falls
they says

Extra ways to have fun with this book

After the reader has finished the story, ask them questions about what they have just read:

What things did Rabbit forget he needed for lunch?
Why did Rabbit need a nap at the end of the story?

Make flashcards of the focus sounds (sh, ch, th, th, ng, nk, le). Ask the reader to say the sounds. This will help reinforce letter/sound matches.

'I'm going, they wouldn't let me read at the table.

A pronunciation guide

This grid highlights the sounds used in the story and offers a guide on how to say them.

s as in sat	a as in ant	t as in tin	p as in pig	i as in ink
n as in net	c as in cat	e as in egg	h as in hen	r as in rat
m as in mug	d as in dog	g as in get	o as in ox	u as in up
l as in log	f as in fan	b as in bag	j as in jug	v as in van
w as in wet	z as in zip	y as in yet	k as in kit	qu as in quick
x as in box	ff as in off	ll as in ball	ss as in kiss	zz as in buzz
ck as in duck	pp as in puppy	nn as in bunny	rr as in arrow	gg as in egg
dd as in daddy	bb as in chubby	tt as in attic	sh as in shop	ch as in chip
th as in them	th as in thin	ng as in sing	nk as in sunk	le as in bottle

Be careful not to add an ‘uh’ sound to ‘s’, ‘t’, ‘p’, ‘c’, ‘h’, ‘r’, ‘m’, ‘d’, ‘g’, ‘l’, ‘f’ and ‘b’. For example, say ‘fff’ not ‘fuh’ and ‘sss’ not ‘suh’.

Rabbit **has** a den. Dog and Rat visit for lunch.

The den is full **of** things, a sink, a kettle, a rug, a jug, pots, pans and cups.

But Rabbit has **no** table!

"**I** forgot. **We need** a table!"

Dog **goes to** the shed. **He** gets thick bits of **wood**. Dog chops it.

But Rabbit has no **chairs**!

“I forgot. We need chairs!”

Rat gets **hay** to sit on.

But Rabbit has no lunch!

“I forgot.
We need lunch!”

Then a leg **falls** off the table!

And bugs from the hay are in the den! Buzz! Buzz! Buzz!

Quick, get out of the den!

They have a picnic for lunch.

It is the best.

"I need a nap,"
says Rabbit.

"I forgot. I need a bed!"

Dog and Rat did not!

OVER 48 TITLES IN SIX LEVELS

Abigail Steel recommends...

Some titles from Level 1
I love reading phonics
Bad Rat
978-1-84898-600-8
I love reading phonics
The Best Gift
978-1-84898-603-9
I love reading phonics
Clint and Grant Play I-Spy
978-1-78325-098-1
I love reading phonics
Gran and Bret's Trip
978-1-78325-100-1

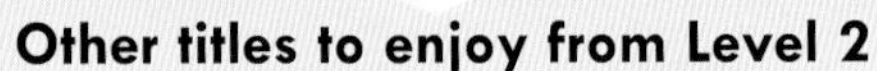

Other titles to enjoy from Level 2

I love reading phonics
Chuck and Duck

978-1-84898-605-3

I love reading phonics
Let's go to the Swings

978-1-78325-102-5

I love reading phonics
Kyle in Trouble

978-1-78325-101-8

Some titles from Level 3

I love reading phonics
Bart's Go-Cart

978-1-78325-105-6

I love reading phonics
Queen Ella's Feet

978-1-84898-609-1

I love reading phonics
Puff Flies

978-1-84898-610-7

I love reading phonics
The Pop Duet

978-1-78325-108-7

An Hachette UK Company
www.hachette.co.uk

First published in Great Britain in 2012 by TickTock, an imprint of Octopus Publishing Group Ltd,
Endeavour House, 189 Shaftesbury Avenue, London WC2H 8JY.
www.octopusbooks.co.uk
www.ticktockbooks.co.uk

ISBN 978 1 78325 104 9

Printed and bound in China
10 9 8 7 6 5 4 3